W9-AVM-131

DISCARD

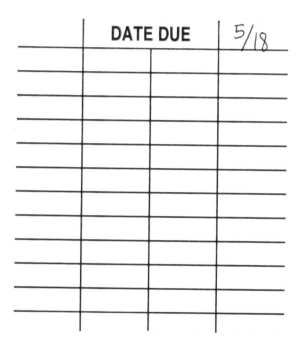

		DATE DUE	5/18

SPINNING
AWAY

BY JAKE MADDOX

text by
Joelle Wisler

STONE ARCH BOOKS
a capstone imprint

Jake Maddox JV Girls books are published by
Stone Arch Books
a Capstone imprint
1710 Roe Crest Drive
North Mankato, Minnesota 56003

www.mycapstone.com

Copyright © 2018 Stone Arch Books

All rights reserved. No part of this publication may be reproduced in whole or in part, or stored in a retrieval system, or transmitted in any form or by any means, electronic, mechanical, photocopying, recording, or otherwise, without written permission of the publisher.

Library of Congress Cataloging-in-Publication Data is available on the Library of Congress website.

ISBN: 978-1-4965-4927-3 (library binding)
ISBN: 978-1-4965-4929-7 (paperback)
ISBN: 978-1-4965-4931-0 (eBook PDF)

Summary: Magnolia and her sister Beatrice are twin sister figure skaters. But when Magnolia tries to break away from the usual program, the sisters and their mother face a difficult situation.

Art Director: Russell Griesmer
Designer: Kayla Rossow
Media Researcher: Wanda Winch
Production Specialist: Tori Abraham

Photo Credits:
Shutterstock: Ann Muse, back cover, chapter openers (background), cluckva, 92-95 (background), Eky Studio, throughout (stripes design), Olga Besnard, cover

Printed and bound in Canada.
010382F17

TABLE OF CONTENTS

CHAPTER 1

THE BIG CHANGE

Magnolia's heart hammered in her chest as she trudged down the spiral staircase into her family's great room. The frowning faces of her ancestors peered out from behind the gold-framed pictures on the wall. Their faces looked as angry as her mother's was sure to be.

Moments before, Magnolia's hair had been blond and almost long enough to sit on. Now it was short and spiky and as blue as a robin's egg. Watching the pale locks float to the floor as she hacked away with a scissors felt wonderful to Magnolia. It was almost as if she had been shedding something that had never really belonged to her.

But now she had to face her mother.

Standing outside the closed kitchen door, Magnolia — no, she decided, it would be just "Maggie" from now on — could hear the murmurings of her family as they prepared breakfast. Her father's voice rumbled low like thunder, but it was her mother's softer but sterner voice that really made the sweat break out on Maggie's palms. She was probably telling Maggie's twin sister, Beatrice, to sit up straight. Her mother was always scolding them about their posture.

In her mind, Maggie could see Beatrice obeying by lifting her chin and straightening her back. Beatrice always did whatever their mother wanted. Beatrice wouldn't complain about the disgusting egg whites and spinach that would surely be sitting on her plate. Breakfast on the mornings of figure-skating competitions always meant egg whites and spinach.

The thought of having to spoon up that white and green slime made Maggie want to barf. She would eat without complaint, though. She was going to be in enough trouble as it was.

Maggie pulled her shoulders back. She thought, *Well, I hope I live to see thirteen.* She nudged open the swinging door and peeked in.

Sunlight streamed into her family's kitchen. It was spotless and flawlessly decorated, just like the rest of their home. Her mother stood pouring coffee, the smell of the roasted beans filling the air. She was also spotless and flawlessly decorated. She wore an all-white outfit with large pearls earrings and fingernails polished perfectly pink. Maggie didn't understand how anybody could ever wear white. She liked ketchup too much.

At first, no one seemed to see Maggie as she entered. Beatrice was in the middle of telling the story about how she had landed her first double axel the day before.

We all know how great you are, Beatrice, Maggie thought. *You can stop rubbing it in.*

Maggie slid into her spot at the table as silent as a ghost. *Yep, egg whites and spinach. Gross.* She held her breath and shoveled a huge bite into her mouth. She followed it with a gulp of orange juice to mask the taste. This would not be what she would have chosen for her last meal on earth.

When Beatrice's voice broke off mid-sentence, the sudden silence pressed in around Maggie's ears. It was more powerful than if a train had decided to roll right through their house. Her gut curdled with fear.

She had been spotted.

Her mother choked out a garbled sound from across the room and then went quiet. When Maggie dared to sneak a look at her from beneath lowered lashes, she saw that her mother's eyes had gone round with horror. Maggie wasn't prepared for the rush of shame that flooded

8

through her. She ran a hand over the spikes on her head.

"I was . . . going for a . . . new look?" she said, her voice sounding small and scared. As if making a peace offering, she started to spoon her breakfast into her mouth again.

Beatrice's mouth gaped like the trout Maggie had caught last summer at their lake cabin. The girls' dad's eyes twinkled and danced with thinly disguised amusement and maybe just a touch of worry.

The door to the kitchen swung as her mother stalked out.

Beatrice shoveled one last bite of breakfast in and threw her napkin on her plate. "Why are you so *weird*, Magnolia?" she said.

"Beatrice," their dad warned. He raised his eyebrows as if to say more but left it at that.

"Seriously," Beatrice said. "I don't know how Magnolia and I are even sisters, let alone twins."

She gave Maggie one last scathing stare and left, flipping her blond ponytail over her shoulder.

"Guess they didn't like your new hairstyle," their dad said. It seemed as if he was trying really hard not to laugh.

Maggie gave him a grateful smile. At least it seemed as if someone was on her side. *It's just hair,* she thought. *What's the big deal?*

* * *

Zoe squealed when she saw Maggie at the skating rink. The two girls hugged. Beatrice rolled her eyes at them.

She's just jealous, Maggie thought, putting down her monogrammed skating bag and opening up her locker. Beatrice spent too much time worrying about how to be a perfect ice skater. She never had any friends.

Zoe's mom owned a hair styling salon, which was how Maggie had gotten the blue dye. Zoe was always showing up to school with crazily colored hair, and she regularly picked out her own clothes at the mall.

Maggie would give anything to do that. Their mother still ordered her and Beatrice to wear matching outfits like they were five years old.

The rest of the team was getting ready for the competition. There was a lot of laughing and chattering in the locker room. As each teammate saw Maggie, they either gave her a high-five or looked at her like she was insane. Maggie didn't care. She felt more like herself than ever.

Giddy from the new feeling, Maggie dug out her skating outfit and grimaced. It was pink, her mother's favorite non-white color. The skirt was lacy and flowing with delicate sleeves that looked like they belonged on a Barbie doll.

Maggie's skates sat on the floor. They were the best skates money could buy. White, of course. She had asked for black skates a couple of years ago for her birthday, but her mother wouldn't even discuss it. And when Maggie had asked to pick her own music, her mother just shook her head and picked out another boring classical song.

Across the locker room, Beatrice stretched. Her blond locks were in a high bun. Not a single strand of hair was out of place. She looked snobbish but comfortable in her skin. Maggie was certain that Beatrice didn't feel the same wild pull inside of her body that Maggie so often felt. The pull tugged at Maggie and told her to do something different. To *be* someone different.

Maggie finished changing. She straightened her ugly pink costume and slid blade protectors over her spotless white skates. As she walked toward the exit of the locker room, she caught a glimpse of her bright blue hair in a mirror. Her heart did a happy little jig. She couldn't believe she'd really done it and had the sudden thought that maybe she should just quit skating altogether.

CHAPTER 2

THE COMPETITION

Maggie picked at her fingernails as she watched Beatrice skate. The popcorn smell from the concession stands made her nervous stomach grumble. She hadn't been able to finish her breakfast after all.

The competition was the last one until regionals, which would determine who'd go to state. Maggie had little hope for her own performance and told herself she didn't care anyway.

Beatrice skated hard, turned, and planted her toe pic. She leapt in the air. Instead of the single axel she usually did, she doubled it.

Maggie couldn't believe it. Beatrice had just learned that move the day before! Up in the stands, their parents stood and cheered. Maggie folded her arms across her chest and frowned.

Maggie and Beatrice were completely identical, all the way down to the mirrored freckles on their noses. The girls' heartbeats had even beaten in sync before they were born. But as identical as they were on the outside, the girls couldn't have been more different on the inside. Beatrice loved everything their mother loved: romantic movies, classical music, and reading quietly. Maggie liked scary movies, rock-n-roll, and wild dancing in her room. Sometimes she wondered if she had been born into the right family.

Beatrice went into her spin combination. Her arms curved above her head in the way their ballet teacher had taught. The music swelled in the air. Beatrice caught her foot in front of her and spun faster, the silver blades of her skates flashing.

Maggie didn't know why she even tried to compete against her sister — Beatrice was so graceful. The back of Maggie's neck felt hot all of a sudden. She was always nervous right before she went on the ice.

The crowd cheered as Beatrice finished her final sit spin. She rose and bowed to them as if she was their queen and they were her royal subjects. She looked so composed and sure of herself that Maggie felt another sharp prickle of jealousy.

Maggie looked around for Coach Bennett, who was usually there to give last minute words of advice. Strangely, she realized she hadn't seen her coach at all that day. Maggie didn't have time to worry, though.

It was her turn.

"You see my double axel?" Beatrice asked, her breath coming out in smoky little puffs from the exertion of her long program. Her eyes gazed with hope at Maggie. Maggie detected smugness.

"Oh, I wasn't really paying attention, Bea," Maggie lied. "Sorry." She didn't know why she didn't want to congratulate her sister. She just couldn't stand how Beatrice thought she was the greatest skater out there.

Beatrice's face fell at Maggie's words.

Maggie shoved down all of her angry feelings and took off her blade protectors. She ruffled her blue hair with one hand and tried to put her sister out of her mind.

The two of them used to do everything together. But then Beatrice had become obsessed with being the best at the same time that Maggie's passion for skating began to dwindle. More and more, they avoided each other at school and at the rink. They seemed to barely tolerate each other during family meals.

The lights burned brightly as Maggie skated out onto the frozen stage. She felt her mother's eyes boring into her, sending icy daggers into the blue hair atop Maggie's head. She wished a portal would just open up. She would jump in and disappear.

Maggie crossed her skates and raised her arms above her head for the starting position. She felt like a tiny puppet that had its strings crossed. It seemed as if she was watching herself from high above the stands. She saw her pink frilly dress and her white skates clash with her blue hair like some mismatched doll.

It wasn't as if Maggie hated everything about skating. She loved the way her muscles bunched and pulled under her skin when she leapt high into the air. She loved spinning so fast that she felt like she was melting right down into the ground like butter. She loved figuring out new ways to do the same old jumps and turns. She frustrated her coach daily because she always wanted to do her own thing instead of practicing a carefully choreographed routine.

When the gentle melody of her song started to play, Maggie had to stifle a groan. It was just so *slow*. The delicate violin music made her want to take a nap, not figure skate. She looked down at her dress. She wished she was wearing something bright and loud, and she wanted rock music blaring in the background.

Maggie had watched the famous U.S. skater Ashley Wagner skate to Pink Floyd's "Shine On You Crazy Diamond" a million times. But whenever she brought up changing her music, her mother always said, "No, Magnolia. If you want to figure skate, you'll do it the proper way."

Maggie's arms and legs began to move, but she felt stiff and mechanical. She felt like the Tin Man from *The Wizard of Oz* as she went into her first spin combination. Her skates slid beneath her awkwardly. She tipped over, her hand grazing the ice for a moment. Her cheeks flushed bright red with embarrassment.

She was able to stumble through her footwork okay, technically, but she did it without any fire. She knew that everyone watching could see that she really didn't want to be out there.

Jumps were up next.

Maggie skated backward, circling around to get into the right position. She approached the spot where she would do her axel-toe loop combination. She'd been struggling with that move for weeks.

She knew she was going too slowly, and she knew that her mark was going to be off. At the last second she tried to pick up the pace, but it was too late. She went into the air for her axel knowing that she wasn't anywhere near as balanced as she needed to be.

She revolved around like an unwilling rag doll. She landed wrong. Her skate slid, and she fell hard onto the ice. Pain shot through her hip and went into her back.

Maggie didn't have time to think.

She pushed herself up from the cold surface. She wanted to salvage the rest of her routine but skated the next minute in a haze.

The music died down. Maggie tried to re-create the ending position, but her left leg was throbbing from her fall. It slipped from underneath her, and she went down, again, onto the ice on one knee.

At last, the violins finally stopped their horrible tune.

Maggie got up and limped off the ice to a smattering of applause. When she dared a quick peek up into the stands, she saw her mother standing there with her arms stiff by her sides. The scowl fixed on her face cut deep grooves in her cheeks.

Maggie ducked her head in shame and plowed onward, almost running right into Beatrice, who was blocking her way.

"That was an interesting program," Beatrice said, her face pinched and mean.

Bright red blotches formed on Maggie's cheeks, and she shoved past her sister. She wanted nothing more than to curl up and hide forever.

CHAPTER 3

THE NEW COACH

The next morning, Beatrice sat in the front of the car and chirped away at their mother. She went over every move from her performance the day before. Their mother still hadn't spoken to Maggie about her hair. The jealousy that Maggie had felt from the day before when Beatrice had won the competition had grown into a giant angry toad squatting in her belly.

Maggie traced lines into the frost of her window and daydreamed about walking into the rink, tossing her skates onto the ice, and never looking back. An image of her mother's disappointed face flashed through her mind.

23

She wished she had the guts to go through with it.

When they arrived at the rink, Beatrice hopped out, as always prepared and excited to get to work. In the back seat, Maggie struggled to make sense of her stuff, frantically jamming warm-ups and skates into her skating bag.

"I want you to know how disappointed I am in your decision to wreck your hair, Magnolia," her mother said. Her voice came calmly from the front of the car.

Maggie looked at the rearview mirror to catch her mother's eye, but her mother stared straight ahead. Maggie got out of the car as quickly as she could. She decided to pretend that her mother hadn't spoken at all. As she stomped up the stairs to the rink, she wished she'd had the guts to say something back to her mother. Inside the locker room, she laced up her skates. As she did, her hands trembled.

No other girls had arrived. She and Beatrice got the most ice time out of anyone and were always at the rink first as their mother insisted. Maggie would have gladly given her time to someone else as it obviously wasn't doing her any good. She'd come in dead last at the competition.

She opened up her backpack, pulling out the pink warm-up sweatshirt that had, until recently, been identical to the one Beatrice was wearing. Maggie had made some alterations to the sweatshirt using some scissors and paint and glittery jewels. The blue swirls she'd painted would look great with her hair. Her mother would probably have to hide all the craft supplies from now on. Maggie snickered to herself.

Maggie waited for Beatrice to leave the locker room wearing her flawless puke-pink warm-up. Then Maggie threw hers on. She took a few minutes in front of a mirror to admire how the bedazzling sparkled as she turned. The rips in the shoulders really added something, too. She was glad in that moment that her mother never stuck around to watch practice anymore.

Maggie made her way out to the rink. She realized quickly that something was wrong. Instead of doing her morning drills, Beatrice was standing all by herself and looking forlorn. Their mother was still there, gesturing and talking loudly with the rink director.

"Hey, Bea, what's going on?" Maggie asked, approaching her sister.

Beatrice looked like she was going to cry. "Coach Bennett quit," she said. She wrapped her arms around herself. "She got a better offer at another rink, I guess."

Despite the selfish shiver of happiness that shot through her own body, Maggie felt bad for Beatrice. She knew how much her sister loved Coach Bennett. Maggie had always had a more difficult relationship with their coach. They had different ideas on how Maggie should be spending her ice time. And they were both stubborn.

"So who's going to take over?" Maggie asked, trying hard not to sound too thrilled.

Beatrice's lower lip quivered. She pointed out to the ice at a man, dressed all in black, who skated like he didn't have a care in the world. He was doing spins and jumps over and over, tiny chips of ice spraying into the air every time he landed. When his hands whipped around, the silver rings on all of his fingers caught the light and winked.

Maggie thought, with a thrill, that if that was their new coach, things were definitely going to be changing.

The man began to skate over to the girls, stopping on the other side of the Plexiglas wall and smiling wide. Maggie noticed that he had a colorful tattoo sleeve that snaked up one arm. Oh, her mother was really not going to like that.

"Hey, girls. You're here early," the man said. He lounged against the wall. He seemed so confident and completely unaware that there was a loud argument happening — *about him* — just a short distance away.

Maggie could feel Beatrice's whole body stiffen beside her. Beatrice would be waiting to see how she should react from their mother.

"We always show up early," Maggie said. "I'm Maggie, and this is my twin sister, Beatrice." She stood up and smoothed down her warm-up. "Are you our new coach?"

"I'm Coach Stone, and I sure *hope* so," he said. He nodded toward the group of adults who were still talking loudly. "But I guess we'll see."

Looking up — way up — at him, Maggie noticed how very tall Coach Stone was. She also noticed a mischievous sparkle in his eyes.

Just then, Maggie's mother appeared, storm clouds in her eyes. "Girls, we are going home," she said, pulling her white gloves out of her designer purse and brushing invisible dust from them. "Go grab your things."

Coach Stone smirked and said, "It was nice meeting you, Maggie and Beatrice."

Maggie's mother walked away without saying a word to him, her heels clicking loudly on the cement floor. Beatrice jumped up and followed her like a mouse.

Maggie sighed and waved limply at Coach Stone, saying, "See ya later." She started to walk to the locker room to change back into her school clothes but then turned and said, "Well, maybe." She didn't have much hope of that, though.

"Hey, Maggie," Coach Stone said.

"Yeah?" said Maggie, looking back at him one last time.

"Nice hair."

CHAPTER 4

COACH STONE'S SURPRISE

In the week since Coach Bennett quit, Maggie and Beatrice hadn't been allowed back to the skating rink. Beatrice had begun to act even more miserable and moody than normal, sulking around the house and snapping when spoken to. Their mother had been trying to get the local skating association to match Coach Bennett's new salary. But she wasn't having any luck. Coach Bennett was happy with the change and wasn't interested in coming back.

Maggie was busy decorating her bedroom ceiling with glow-in-the-dark stars. One of her dad's favorite Rolling Stones songs blasted out from the speakers in her room. Maggie placed another sticker above her head and then jumped around on her mattress, playing air guitar like a rock star.

Just then, her door swung open with a bang and there stood Beatrice, looking like she could spit fire. "What did you do, Magnolia?" Beatrice shouted over the music. She brandished her bright red headphones in the air like an angry flag.

"Nothing?" said Maggie, sitting down on her bed and picking at the threads of her comforter nervously. She had lost her own headphones the week before. While borrowing Beatrice's, she'd accidentally spilled a glass of water on them. She'd been hoping her sister wouldn't notice.

"You never take care of your stuff, Magnolia," said Beatrice.

She picked up Maggie's torn and bedazzled sweatshirt that was lying on a chair. "If you don't lose something, you wreck it by cutting it up into pieces."

Maggie shrugged.

"And now you're ruining all of my stuff too," said Beatrice, her voice slowly approaching the sound only dogs could hear. "And, by the way, you look completely and utterly crazy with your messed-up hair."

"You're just mad about Coach Bennett," said Maggie.

Beatrice threw her headphones down, and they bounced on the floor. She glared at Maggie. "Don't . . . touch . . . my . . . stuff."

With that, she stomped out of the room, slamming Maggie's door behind her. Beatrice's elephant-like feet pound down the hallway, followed by a shrill call of, "MO-OM!"

Maggie cringed.

Being in even more trouble was just what she needed. She flopped down onto her bed, closed her eyes, and tried to let the music take her to a different place. She pretended that she was doing a perfect Biellman spin, her leg stretched out behind her. She could feel the arch in her back and the ice beneath her skate as she whirled in a perfectly spun circle. Her parents were going crazy in the stands.

Maggie smiled to herself.

The first couple of days without skating had been pure bliss for Maggie. She'd slept in and been able to come home right after school. She'd even gotten all of her homework done with time left over to read for fun.

Slowly, though, it had begun to feel like bugs were crawling underneath her skin. Having all the extra time had ultimately become boring. She'd started to actually miss skating. She missed the cold air at the rink, no matter the temperature outside. She missed making patterns on the ice with newly sharpened blades.

The spinning, though — she missed the spinning most of all.

Maggie missed twirling so fast that no one could see her face. She became someone different when she spun. Not Magnolia, Beatrice's twin sister. Not her mother's daughter, who always had to be perfect. She became simply Maggie.

* * *

Maggie's dad walked in the door from work. He sat down at the dinner table and started to pile pot roast onto his plate, smiling away at his family.

"How's life for my three sunshines?" he said.

He started to whistle. He was almost always in a good mood. It was as if her parents had been allotted only one person's happiness, and her dad was the one who got it. He was a bit oblivious to any drama in the house, but Maggie loved that.

Maggie's mother set her fork next to her plate. She looked up and had dark circles under her eyes "Well, girls," she said all of a sudden, "your father and I have made a decision." She gave her husband a squint-eyed look. He stopped his whistling and straightened up, sensing that he needed to look serious.

Maggie's fork, filled with mashed potatoes, paused mid-flight. She looked over at her dad. He gave her a thumbs-up. She felt like there were bees buzzing around in her stomach.

"Do we get to skate again?" Beatrice asked, her face lighting up like the belly of a lightning bug.

"Well, we are going to talk with . . . Coach Stone," their mother said. She choked out his name as if it tasted bad in her mouth. "Tonight, actually. He's coming over." She paused and stared right at Maggie. "So we'll need you two to go do your homework right after dinner."

"But we already did it," Beatrice said.

Maggie kicked her hard under the table.

"Ow!" said Beatrice.

"We have that other project . . . in science, remember, Bea?" Maggie said. She smiled big and then widened her eyes at Beatrice. "We have *loads* to do."

Beatrice frowned at Maggie but didn't say another word. Maggie sure wished that they had that creepy twin telepathy sometimes. After dinner the girls went to their rooms like their mother had asked.

They'd only been in their rooms for a short period of time when Maggie heard the doorbell. She tiptoed out of her room and tapped on Beatrice's door and beckoned her out into the hallway. Despite being clueless at dinner, Beatrice seemed to catch on.

The two girls found a spot at the top of the stairs where they could stay invisible but see and hear what was happening.

It felt like one of those late nights when they were little and had snuck out to take in one of their parents' parties.

They had to squeeze together in the tight spot, their legs piling up on top of each other. Maggie thought that it felt good to be on the same team as Beatrice for once. The thought made her so happy that a giggle bubbled up inside of her, and she snorted.

Beatrice elbowed her. "Shhh," she said. "He's talking now."

Coach Stone had worn a suit and tie — no tattoos in sight. Maggie gave him a high-five for effort in her mind. It sounded like he was talking about his education and all of the places he'd worked before.

And then Coach Stone finished his last sentence with the words, "and then for the past two years, I've been working at the Olympic Training Center."

The breath whooshed out of Maggie at once.
She looked over at Beatrice, whose eyes bulged
in shock. Maggie felt like she had a marching
band drumming through her veins. Coach Stone
had worked at the United States Olympic
Training Center.

Surely their mother would have to approve of
him now.

CHAPTER 5

MAGGIE FINDS HER MAGIC

Maggie stood next to her mother inside the arena. Her mother's breath puffed out like a dragon's in the cold air. The effect gave her face a scary quality.

"Nothing has changed, Magnolia," her mother said.

Maggie cringed at hearing her full name.

Her mother stared straight ahead, her back as straight as the ironing board she spent so much time with. "We're going to stick with your normal routine and the classical music."

41

How did she know what I was thinking? Maggie thought to herself.

She had just been day-dreaming about ice-skating. Led Zeppelin had been playing in the background in her fantasy, and she was wearing a dark purple velvet skating outfit with rhinestones. She imagined doing a double axel just like Beatrice — but looking way cooler than Beatrice while doing it.

"Okay, Mom," Maggie said, feeling the familiar sadness whenever her mother put her foot down. Having tried many times before, Maggie knew that it was useless to argue.

Five minutes later, Maggie's mother was up in the stands. All of the other skaters were laced up and standing on the ice, shivering a bit. Coach Stone skated toward them. He turned backward and started picking up speed. He steadied himself before swinging his right leg up, sending him flying into the air.

One, two, three and a half turns. A triple axel.

All the girls gasped and started to clap.

Maggie couldn't believe it. That was the most amazing jump she'd ever seen in person. Butterflies floated inside of her. No other coach of hers had ever done anything like that.

As he landed and skated over to the group, Coach Stone's grin spread across his face.

"Good morning, young skaters," he said, planting one skate across the other and leaning onto the railing. "Before we begin," he continued, making sure that he directed his gaze at each girl individually, "I want to repeat for our two new athletes, Maggie and Beatrice, what I told the rest of you last week."

The girls all gave knowing smiles to the twins.

Maggie glanced up anxiously at the stands toward her mother, who was watching closely but was probably too far away to hear Coach Stone's words.

Coach Stone pushed off the Plexiglas wall with his hands. He said, "I believe that skating should be, most of all . . ." He spun around with his limbs flying in all directions. "Fun." He finished his move and raised his arms high above his head. He waggled his eyebrows.

Many of the girls started to laugh. Maggie fidgeted with the tips of her gloves.

"Let's get started," Coach Stone said. He skated over toward the stereo system and pushed a button. Pulsing music began to pump out the arena speakers, seemingly on all sides of them. "Today, I want you all to just skate. Forget about what you're *supposed* to do. Move to the music."

Maggie felt her feet come alive. They slid back and forth to the rhythm of the song. She began to tap her hands on the tops of her thighs.

The rest of the girls gawked at each other, willing someone to do something first. Under Coach Bennett, they'd always been told to practice specific skills before. They did warm-ups, then drills, then new skills. It was always the same. They weren't quite sure what to do with their brand new freedom.

Beatrice looked completely confused. She kept glancing up at their mother. Maggie knew how much Beatrice liked to have a plan, a checklist of activities. A plus B equaled C. A logical sequence.

Finally, Zoe beamed at Maggie and started to move out onto the ice. She shot her hands into the air like she'd just been attacked by the music. She'd already spent a full week practicing with Coach Stone and was clearly more familiar with his odd techniques.

Maggie chuckled out loud and decided right then that she wasn't even going to look in her mother's direction. In fact, she wasn't going to think about her at all. She was going to follow her feet, which seemed to be skating around in a circle all by themselves. She moved her hips from side to side and twirled, letting the music flow into her blood, her muscles, her limbs.

Now this I could skate to, Maggie thought as she began to fly across the ice, kicking her feet up and feeling all of her cells bounce to the music. It felt amazing. She began to skate faster, turning right at the last moment before she plowed into the wall. Then she went into her combination sit spin, crossing her arms in front of her, leaving perfect circles carved into the ice below.

Maggie stood up and skated hard, moving into an axel and then a double toe loop. It all seemed *so easy* as her body took over. She glided across the ice, avoiding the other skaters as they loosened up, moving and jumping and spinning to the beat. Most of the girls seemed to be having as much fun as she was.

Maggie ignored them as she leapt and shimmied and skated. Her muscles felt incredibly strong and sure. All of her hours of training seemed to click right into place. *This is what Beatrice feels*, she thought with amazement. *This is why she's so good at skating.*

The peak of the song was coming up. Maggie skated backward, her feet crisscrossing. There was an open space on the ice, and she wanted to try another axel. Actually, she was feeling so confident that she wanted to attempt a double axel. She'd tried to pull it off before but never had done it.

Maggie sped across the ice and jumped into the air. She completed the normal axel rotation and then the full extra revolution before landing just as the music slowed down.

Maggie couldn't believe it — she'd just landed her very first double axel. Her heart pounded to the bass line of the song, and she spun around and around with the dying notes, not wanting the feeling to end. As she slowed, she started to realize that the rest of the skaters had stopped. They were staring at her, mouths hanging open.

Beatrice glowered at Maggie. Their mother sat as still as a tombstone, pursing her lips.

Maggie wrapped her arms around herself. *What just happened?* she thought. *Did I really just land a double axel?*

* * *

As Maggie lay in her bed that night, she overheard her parents talking. Her mother used words like "unbalanced" and "outlandish" and "bizarre" to describe Coach Stone and his methods. Her father asked questions but didn't put up much of a defense.

When Maggie finally fell asleep, she tossed and turned with strange visions. In one, Coach Stone leapt into the air, and then the snake tattoo on his arm came to life and hissed at Maggie that she would never be as good as her sister.

The next morning, Maggie felt her mother shaking her shoulder gently.

"Hey, sleepyhead," her mother said.

She stroked Maggie's forehead.

Maggie looked out her window and saw that the worried face of the moon was still shining into her room. The sky was still pitch black.

"What time is it?" Maggie asked. She rubbed her eyes, trying to make sense of what was happening.

"It's early," her mother said, "but we're driving the hour to train with Coach Bennett from now on." She patted Maggie's leg and then, as if an afterthought, "If Beatrice wants to make regionals, she really needs to get back on the ice with someone more traditional."

Even though Maggie's brain wasn't quite awake enough to process that information, her stomach dropped. She had known she hadn't had much of a shot to make regionals herself, but it was crushing to hear it come directly from her mother's mouth. Maggie noticed there was also no mention of what Maggie wanted or needed.

Her mother walked out of Maggie's bedroom. Seconds later, she heard Beatrice staggering to the bathroom. Maggie moaned and pulled the covers up around her head. Her mother had officially lost her mind.

In the car, Maggie's mother explained to her daughters that they would to continue to train with their ballet and jump coaches after school in their old rink, but every morning they'd go to Coach Bennett's.

Beatrice soon fell asleep beside Maggie. She looked peaceful, knowing that she would get to train with her old coach again.

While Maggie watched her sister's steady breathing, she felt like her own heart was breaking. Just the day before, she had experienced a passion for skating she'd never felt before. She'd gotten only the smallest dose, but now it was being taken away because her mother couldn't handle "unusual."

The drive to Coach Bennett's new skating rink was an hour long one way. That meant a two-hour round trip each day. Maggie wasn't sure what was worse: the dreariness, how tired she was, or worrying that she was going to be that tired every single morning — maybe the rest of her life.

Maggie decided that things really couldn't be worse. Her mother had made a decision and didn't care what anybody else thought about it.

CHAPTER 6

DECISIONS

Over the next period of time, Maggie's entire family grew more and more short-tempered. Instead of greeting each other with, "Good morning," they simply grunted. The puffy circles under her mother's eyes were so large they began to resemble bean bag chairs. The long hours in the car were wretched. And training with Coach Bennett made Maggie feel like she was getting painted into the wrong picture all over again.

At practice one morning, Maggie collided with Beatrice from behind. Both girls fell down onto the ice.

"Watch it, Magnolia!" Beatrice hollered, rubbing her elbow.

"You watch it," Maggie snapped, shoving her sister's leg off of her own. It wasn't fair, Beatrice getting everything she wanted. She *always* got everything she wanted just because she liked the same things their mother liked.

As Maggie went to stand up, she slid a bit. The blade of her skate slipped forward and caught the tender skin on her sister's shin. They both watched in horror as blood quickly welled up and soaked through Beatrice's white tights.

"Oh no, Bea," Maggie said, placing her own gloved hand over the cut, panicking. "I'm so sorry."

Tears pooled in the corner of Beatrice's eyes, but she didn't let them escape. She got up and skated slowly over to Coach Bennett. Years of figure skating had taught them both to be brave when injured.

It was one thing they had in common, at least.

Maggie felt terrible about hurting her sister. She was so exhausted. She couldn't skate or even *think* straight. Something had to change.

Maggie slipped away to the locker room and kicked off her skates. She collapsed onto the wooden bench and dropped her head into her hands. Her dad's face popped into her mind. She needed someone on her side.

* * *

Maggie waited until Beatrice and her mother went to bed. Then she crept to the study and opened the door. Inside, it smelled like a mixture of wood and leather and her dad's aftershave. It made her feel like a small child again.

Her dad looked up from his papers. "What's up Magnolia?" he asked. "I mean, Maggie."

Maggie loved him for remembering what she wanted to be called.

"Can I talk to you for a second?" she asked. She walked over and curled up in one of his dark brown chairs.

He got up and came to sit in the chair beside her. He grabbed both of her hands and squeezed them. "It's about the ice skating situation, right?"

The concern on his face caused tears to spring suddenly to Maggie's eyes. She found herself blurting out the story of her one day of practice with Coach Stone. She talked and talked. She told him all about how she'd felt so free and alive.

"Mom is being so unfair," Maggie said. "She never cares about what I want." She lowered her head, snot and tears now running down her face in a steady stream.

Her dad reached up to wipe her face with his handkerchief.

"I want to tell you a story, Maggie," he said in a serious voice. "This is a story about your mom that you might not have heard before."

Maggie thought she knew everything about her mother.

"When your mom was young, about your age actually," he started, leaning back in his chair, settling into his tale, "she wanted *desperately* to be a figure skater."

"What?" said Maggie.

"Yep," her dad said. "She practiced and practiced." He grinned. "You know how dedicated she can be when she sets her mind to something."

Maggie coughed out a laugh. She did know.

"And then, one day," he continued, "she was in a car accident with her parents."

Maggie blinked rapidly. She had never heard about any car accident.

"She broke her leg," her dad continued. "She broke it so badly, it turned out, that she couldn't skate anymore." He got up from his chair and then sat back down again like he wasn't sure how to finish the story.

"Couldn't she just go to physical therapy?" Maggie said, thinking about all the times she or Beatrice had gone to PT for various injuries.

"Therapy wasn't like it is today, Maggie," he said. "Her leg was never quite the same. That may be why she's so determined to give you girls what she couldn't have." He stopped then, letting the words sink in. He pulled Maggie close for a hug.

As she held onto her dad, the charmed image she'd always had of her mother wavered and floated away. In its place appeared a young girl with a long white cast on her leg. It didn't excuse her mother's behavior. Still, the new image made Maggie feel terrible.

"Thanks for telling me that, Dad," Maggie said. "It helps."

"Sure, Maggie," he said. "Remember that you can talk to her, too. You can let her know how you're feeling."

Maggie nodded and headed upstairs to bed.

Before she turned out the light, she glanced over and saw a photo of Beatrice and herself from the summer before at their grandparents' house. They were wearing matching blue shorts and white shirts. With their matching blond hair, they appeared as identical as could be.

Studying the photo closely, Maggie noticed the strained smile on her own face and remembered how annoyed she'd been that day. She remembered not wanting to take yet another picture of them looking like the same person.

Maggie decided that maybe it was time to give her mother a break. Her mother deserved it. She had never gotten the chance to follow her own skating dreams. As she drifted off to sleep, Maggie caressed the fading blue spikes on her head. Maybe someday she could be who she wanted. But maybe not yet.

CHAPTER 7

SURRENDER

Each day, Maggie and Beatrice drove with their mother to the ice skating rink and went to school. That was it. Between that and the long drive to practice with Coach Bennett, they didn't have time for other outside activities. The pile of snacks and homework in the back of their minivan began to feel like a symbol for Maggie's jumbled-up life.

Beatrice was happier. She had fallen into her all-too-familiar role of being Coach Bennett's star. Maggie watched every morning as they went through the details of Beatrice's routine.

Beatrice had the amazing ability to mimic each new move she was taught without any fear or hesitation. Coach Bennett praised Beatrice's accomplishments. They were an ideal team.

Maggie, on the other hand, couldn't seem to make Coach Bennett proud of anything she did. She continued to skate technically okay, but she just didn't care that much, despite her resolve to try harder for her mother. Her lack of fire showed with each half-hearted leap and turn. Even worse, when spinning, Maggie had occasional flashbacks to the one practice with Coach Stone when she felt like she had magic in her skates. In those moments, when she folded her body into the tiniest ball and spun faster and faster, her heart tripped in her chest like it was getting ready to come alive again.

But then Coach Bennett's voice would growl, "Point your toe, Magnolia! Tuck tighter!" and the spell would break. Maggie would slow her spin, and her heart would continue on with its normal, sleepy rhythm in time with the uninspiring music.

When she felt frustrated, Maggie forced herself to think of her mother as a girl, her leg ruined, heartbroken knowing that she couldn't skate anymore. She owed it to her mother to try and squish herself into that mold that was expected of her. Besides, she just didn't have the energy to fight anymore. Her hair was growing out, and the blue was almost completely washed away. She had even stopped insisting that everyone call her Maggie. She was back to Magnolia.

* * *

"Does your sister want to come sit with us?" Zoe asked one day at lunch. She pointed to Beatrice, who was sitting all alone at the next table over.

"She's not really talking to me right now," Maggie said, opening up her lunch bag from home with a sense of dread.

She reached in and pulled out a strange-looking sandwich. *Was that a carrot in there? With peanut butter?*

Since they'd begun their early morning drives, the girls had been finding odd combinations in their lunch boxes. Their mother was usually half-asleep herself when she packed them. One day, Beatrice had gone to school with just a can of beans and an empty yogurt container.

Maggie slid the carrot out of her sandwich and licked off the peanut butter. *Huh, not bad.* She peered over at Beatrice who had her new headphones on and was doodling in a notebook. *I suppose that she's probably mapping out her new routine or designing another ugly, frilly skating outfit,* Maggie thought.

Beatrice had a one-track mind when it came to ice skating.

"Beatrice is so strange," said Frankie, another girl at the table.

Maggie was caught off-guard by the sudden flash of anger that swooped in. "Just leave her alone, Frankie," she snapped. She smoothed her hair. "She's just a really good skater. If she focuses, our coach said she could maybe make it to Junior Worlds next year."

"Okay. Well, whatever," Frankie said. Her face turned into the color of an overripe eggplant. She turned and started whispering to the girl on the other side of her.

When their giggles erupted a second later, Maggie nearly lost it. She wanted desperately to throw her weird peanut butter sandwich at them. Finally, the girls left the table.

As Maggie calmed down, she realized that she didn't know what had just come over her. She, herself, could think Beatrice was an oddball. Sometimes she even said so. But she decided that she didn't want anyone else talking poorly about her sister.

That night, after begging their mother again to let them get hot lunch at school, Maggie, Beatrice, and their mother stopped at the grocery store to pick up some supplies.

Maggie headed off to the chip aisle right away, hoping that she could sneak some salty contraband into her mother's cart. Turning the corner, she barreled right into the torso of a very large person wearing a black T-shirt.

"Sorry!" Maggie blurted.

When she looked up, she saw Coach Stone. He smiled at her like they were some sort of long lost friends.

"Maggie!" he said.

"Hi, Coach Stone," Maggie mumbled. She glanced around to make sure her mother or Beatrice weren't anywhere near. That would have been even more embarrassing.

"How's skating practice going?" Coach Stone said, his face friendly and open.

"Oh," Maggie said, "okay."

She studied the chip labels on the shelf. She acted like they were the most interesting things in the world. She knew that she wasn't being very convincing.

Seeing Coach Stone made Maggie feel sad. The ache of wanting to have him as a coach almost felt like a wiggly tooth that she couldn't reach.

"Coach Bennett is just . . . really great," Maggie said. She felt like her tongue had forgotten how to function.

"Maggie," Coach Stone said, placing his hand on her shoulder.

Maggie jerked her eyes up to meet his. "Yeah?" she squeaked. She sounded just like mousy Beatrice, which bothered her.

"You've got something really special in you, Maggie," Coach Stone said. "Don't let anyone take that away." He smiled a sad little smile and patted her shoulder one last time.

All Maggie could do was stare.

Coach Stone turned and walked away, humming a tuneless song.

Maggie stood stunned in the chip aisle. A river of tears ran down her face.

CHAPTER 8

ROCK-N-ROLL

Maggie crept downstairs at midnight to get a glass of water.

A light shone beneath the kitchen door. She paused when she realized that her parents were behind the door, talking in hushed voices. She distinctly heard her mother say "Magnolia."

Maggie automatically crouched down before she realized that crouching wasn't going to exactly hide her if her parents left the kitchen. Feeling silly, she stood up again and pressed her ear against the door.

"The driving back and forth is making our lives more complicated than it needs to be," her dad said.

"I know," her mother said, her voice calm. "And you should have seen Magnolia's face. She looked absolutely crushed."

Maggie realized that her mother was talking about that afternoon. After her encounter with Coach Stone, Maggie had run to the grocery store bathroom and splashed her face with cold water to cover up the tearstains. She'd hoped her mother hadn't noticed, but clearly her mother had.

"I think we should let her practice with Coach Stone again," her dad said. "I don't think we gave him enough of a chance."

Maggie crossed her fingers and her toes and squeezed her eyes shut. She wished with every part of her body that her mother would agree.

After a long pause her mother exhaled and said, "I'm still not sure."

Without thinking, Maggie pushed open the door to the kitchen. Her parents both turned toward her in surprise.

"Magnolia, what are you doing out of bed?" her mother asked.

Maggie blushed and said, "I was thirsty, and then I heard you guys talking about me, and . . . " She wasn't sure how to continue.

Caught off-guard, neither of her parents seemed to know what to say, either.

Feelings of hope, fear, and courage swirled in Maggie. She decided in a flash that she had nothing to lose. "Mom, I'm your daughter, but I'm not like exactly you," she said. "I'm never going to be exactly like you. I love crazy music and having blue hair and breaking the rules while skating." Maggie took in a deep breath and continued. "I am the exact opposite of Beatrice, and I love her and you, but I can't *be* her or you."

Her parents stood stock-still.

Maggie felt the weight of her words float throughout the room. She searched desperately for a glimpse of understanding from her mother. "Please understand," Maggie said. "Please."

Her father looked at her mother. Her mother looked at her father.

Finally, her mother came over to her daughter. She took Maggie's face in her hands and kissed her forehead. "Okay," she said.

* * *

Maggie hugged her mother when she dropped her off at Coach Stone's rink the next morning. "Thank you so much," she said.

Her mother drew her in tight like she'd done when Maggie was a little girl. Her mother smelled like perfume and gum and something else that was just uniquely her.

They locked eyes, and her mother said, "I really just want you to be happy, Magnolia."

Beatrice pouted in the back seat.

She was still going to train with Coach Bennett, at least until the next competition. After that, they would figure out if they wanted to continue on. Beatrice was used to getting her way, and she didn't understand why Maggie was getting special treatment.

"Bye, Beatrice," Maggie taunted before she closed the door. "Have a fun drive!"

Beatrice stared straight ahead.

Maggie wiggled her fingers in a wave and then tried to push down the voice inside that told her she was being a brat. She went inside the arena, dressed, and made her way out to the rink.

Coach Stone shook Maggie's hand like she was a grownup. "Great to have you back," he said.

"It's great to be back, Coach," said Maggie. She skated out onto the ice to start her warm-ups.

Bass pounded from the loudspeaker. Other girls were already warmed up and practicing jumps.

Colorful skirts flew in a frenzy. Maggie, however, saw beauty and order in the frenzy. She'd never been so excited to be at practice.

Coach Stone stopped Maggie while she was practicing her sit spin. She was breathless from the effort of trying to maintain a perfect position. She'd always felt, somehow, that spinning was her secret weapon. Practicing in front of Coach Stone had made her want to try even harder.

"What's up, Coach?" Maggie said.

"We're going to work on putting a harder spin combination into your routine," Coach Stone said. He began to skate, showing off his fancy footwork. Coach Stone was always on the ice with his students, always skating. He seemed to love figure skating more than anyone Maggie had ever known, even Beatrice.

"I'm thinking a camel to a Biellman," said Coach Stone. "You have the flexibility, and I think you should try."

Maggie felt needles of doubt in her chest. The Biellman spin was an upright spin where the skater grabbed the foot behind their head. When Maggie thought about trying that, she felt unsure but tried not to let it show in her face. "Do you think I'm ready for that?" Maggie asked.

"I know you're ready," Coach Stone said. He hit the top of the wall hard with his hand, jolting her out of her daydream. "But we better get to work if we want it ready for the competition."

Maggie had seen that spin combination done a thousand times by more experienced skaters. At that moment, for the first time, she couldn't help but begin to imagine exactly how it would feel. The move seemed to be calling to her in a way that she couldn't ignore. She practiced it with Coach Stone for a good portion of the practice.

The next days passed in a blur of happiness for Maggie.

Training with Coach Stone was everything she'd dreamt of. He listened to her ideas and didn't think they were crazy at all. He called her creative and inventive instead of stubborn.

But Coach Stone was also tough — tougher even than Coach Bennett. Maggie had to take ice baths every night to soothe her sore and aching muscles from all the extra work. She was having so much fun on the ice, though, that she didn't seem to mind.

CHAPTER 9

MAGGIE ON STAGE

Maggie had been working relentlessly on her brand new routine. She knew her mother wasn't going to be thrilled with all of the details. If she pulled it off, though, her mother would finally see that different could be great, too.

Maggie was going to skate to a rock-n-roll song, and she was going to be doing some footwork and spins that she'd created herself. But she had been spending most of her time practicing her new difficult spin combination.

Her back and arms were sore and tired from falling over and over onto the hard ice, but she had never felt more alive. The puzzle pieces were finally coming together.

The night before the competition, Maggie was scooting her peas around her plate. Her knees couldn't seem to stop bouncing up and down under the table. She hoped that she was ready, but she wasn't entirely sure. She'd become unbalanced during the Biellman spin earlier that day, and she was scared of the same thing happening when she was in front of hundreds of people. The nerves were beginning to peck their way under her skin and make a nasty little nest.

"Are you girls excited for tomorrow?" their dad boomed suddenly, and the girls both startled.

The tension between the sisters seemed to be escalating the closer it came to the competition. Never before did it seem so much like they were competing *against* each other.

That night, the air felt thick enough to slice with a sword.

"Sure, Dad," both girls muttered at the exact same time, avoiding each other's eyes.

"Wow," he said. "Sure sounds like it. "He caught Maggie's eye. "I'm excited to see what you and Coach Stone have been cooking up."

Beatrice spun her head to look at Maggie so hard she almost got whiplash. "Are you doing something new?"

"Guess you'll have to just wait and see," Maggie said. She got up to scrape her uneaten food into garbage. She didn't want to talk about her routine in front of her mother who was finally being nice to her.

Her mother sat calmly, spearing her broccoli.

* * *

Maggie woke up extra early the next morning. She yawned and stretched.

She spotted a strange package sitting on top of her desk. Picking up the card that lay on top of a package wrapped in shiny gold foil paper, she read, *Good Luck Maggie,* in her dad's familiar sloppy scrawl. Maggie ripped the package open, shredded paper flying, and looked inside to see the most beautiful skating outfit that ever existed. It was royal blue velvet with black leather cap sleeves and metal studs and rhinestones trailing up and down. It oozed rock-n-roll.

Maggie picked it up and crushed it to her chest, thrilled. When she did that, she heard a loud, "clunk" by her feet. Looking down, she burst out laughing when she saw a fresh bottle of blue hair dye with a note taped to it saying, *Just in case,* with a smiley face.

* * *

Beating drums started before the first notes of music began. Maggie tapped her skate to the tempo.

She hoped that her newly shorn and brightly colored hair looked every bit as awesome as it felt. Every move in her routine was burned into her brain, but she mentally ran through her spin combination one more time. Here at the competition, every movement would have to be perfect.

When the loud guitar riff slammed out of the speakers, Maggie flung her arms into the air and dashed across the ice in a complicated sequence of steps that she choreographed. She could feel everyone watching her. She wanted to bring the music to life.

Her first jump combination, a single axel and then a toe loop, went off without a hitch. When Maggie landed exactly on a pause in the music, she could tell that the crowd was holding its breath. Starting across the ice again, her body moved like it was lit from within. Every muscle was alive and in tune with the music.

Maggie launched into a sit-spin and stood up again to carve out a delicate arabesque, the lights pulsing all around her. Her difficult spin combination was coming up. To win, she knew she'd have to nail her final spin and her axel.

Maggie gathered speed and went into the camel spin, lifting her leg behind her as she spun in tight circles. After four rotations, she switched feet to go into the Biellman, arching back gracefully and raising her foot behind her. She was as graceful as Beatrice, as rock-n-roll as Coach Stone, and as confident as she'd ever been.

She spun faster and faster. As she orbited around feeling every fiber in her body, she made her final decision. She was going to double her last axel. She knew that it was a daring decision. She knew that there were many other double jumps in-between that were easier than the double axel. But her mind was made up.

The combination spin came to end.

The crowd cheered, knowing she'd just set the bar higher for the other competitors. Maggie charged down the ice, determined to pick up enough speed for her big jump. She surged ahead, her feet light and nimble.

Turning around, she sped backward and gained power. She took to the air. Maggie soared up and up like a winged thing, higher than she had ever gone before. The two and a half rotations of the axel were almost too easy, and she came down to earth just as the last guitar note screamed.

Maggie halted in her final position with her chest heaving and sweat trickling down her face.

When Maggie looked up, the stands erupted in a shower of cheers. She felt suspended on a cloud of happiness. Her parents whooped and hollered. Coach Stone looked on with pride. Maggie knew then that she'd probably just won the competition. But then she looked to her sister. Beatrice's face was a stormy sea.

CHAPTER 10

SISTERS

Maggie was supposed to be sound asleep, but instead she was reliving every moment of the competition. That included standing on the podium to receive her first-place medal while Beatrice stood below her at second. Maggie had done it, and she had done it her way. As she flipped through each delicious memory, one tiny thought continued to niggle at her like a sliver that she just couldn't remove.

She kept coming back to Beatrice.

Beatrice had acted graciously at the celebratory dinner with their family that night.

Still, Maggie couldn't forget the look on Beatrice's face right after Maggie had finished her routine.

Maggie couldn't stand it anymore. She peeled her comforter off and snuck down the hall to her sister's room. She slid open the door and peered in at Bea's shadowed form on the bed. Beatrice turned when she saw the light from the doorway shining in.

"Scoot over," Maggie said and crawled under the warm sheets next to her sister. Beatrice hiccupped. Her shoulders shivered.

"Are you crying?" Maggie asked, astonished. Beatrice never cried, even when hurt. She was always strong and composed.

"I don't know why I feel so sad," Beatrice said. Her breath was stinky, but Maggie didn't have the heart to tell her that.

"I do," Maggie said. "I always feel a tiny bit bad for myself when you win." She rested her head on Beatrice's damp shoulder, thinking guiltily about how she hadn't even congratulated Beatrice after the last competition. "And you win, like, all the time, you know." Maggie shoved her sister's shoulder, trying to lighten the mood.

"You're just so brave," Beatrice said. "I always wish I could be more like you." Her body shook.

"What?" Maggie said. She seized her sister's hand. "Are you kidding me? You are the most talented skater I know. You try *everything* without even thinking about it. You're the brave one."

"I just do whatever Mom and Coach Bennett say, without even questioning them," Beatrice said. "*You* turned your hair blue!" She was laughing and crying at the same time.

"Well, I don't know if turning my hair blue was brave," Maggie said. "I did it because I felt like I was always in your shadow." Maggie sighed and snuggled up close. "It was my way of shouting, I guess."

Beatrice leaned into Maggie. "I feel like we've been growing apart, and I don't like it. I want us to be friends again. And teammates."

"Me, too," said Maggie. She held onto to Beatrice's hand as if were a life preserver.

Beatrice stopped shaking at last.

Maggie had a flash of insight and yelled, "Bea!"

"Oh, my gosh. What?" Beatrice said, startled.

Now it was Maggie's turn to shake — with laughter. "I have the best idea."

* * *

Early Saturday morning, the girls sat in front of the television, chortling to themselves. They had served themselves big bowls of cereal and then piled onto the couch in a sea of blankets to watch cartoons like they used to. Maggie thought it felt so good to have her sister back, but she was a little freaked out about her mother waking up and seeing what they had done.

An hour later, their mother walked in. "Good morning, girls," she said. She looked mother-like in her fancy silk robe, but her eyes were half-closed. She clung to her cup of coffee like it was vital to her existence.

The girls shared a sly look, wondering when she would notice.

"What are you girls watching?" their mother said, sitting down in chair across from them and finally really looking at them. At Beatrice, especially.

A tense moment passed.

"No," she finally said, shaking her head in disbelief. "Not you, too." Beatrice now had a long blue streak in her blond hair, right in the front.

"Do you like it?" Beatrice asked, trying not to sound scared. Their mother paused for a long time, peering at her two daughters.

"Actually," their mother said, sighing, "I kind of do. But I'm starting to think that we need to make more frequent trips to the salon?" Her eyes gleamed.

The three of them stared at each other and then burst into howling laughter, gripping their sides until they couldn't breathe anymore.

"What's going on down here, you lunatics?" their dad said, entering the living room, looking unshaven and tired.

As the laughter died down, the sisters gave each other a hug. Maggie grabbed Beatrice's hand and said, "We've made a decision."

"What's that?" their dad said, looking at their mother for clues. Their mother shrugged her shoulders.

"We only want to continue to figure skate if we can do it together," Beatrice said. "Here, with Coach Stone. No more driving."

"Oh, thank heavens," their mother said, falling over in a mock faint. "I'm so tired of that stupid drive." The girls watched her in shock, both wondering about the strange new relaxed creature that their mother had become.

Their dad just smiled.

"Now that that's finally settled, how about some music?" their dad said. He walked over to the stereo and pressed some buttons.

Instantly, a loud burst of rock-n-roll music shouted from the speakers. Their dad grabbed their mother, who protested. When he was finally able to pull her up from the chair, he whirled her around until she got so dizzy she fell into him.

Maggie and Beatrice both stood up. The strength of their smiles could have powered the house.

And then they started to spin, together.

Joelle Wisler is a freelance writer and physical therapist. She grew up in South Dakota and is a lifelong runner, jumper, bender, and skier. She spends much of her time these days laughing at her husband and chasing her two kids around — and any stray moose that might wander into her backyard in the mountains of Colorado.

GLOSSARY

apprehension—anxiety or fear that something bad or unpleasant will happen

axel—a jump with a forward outside-edge takeoff and one and a half rotations in the air named after Norwegian skater Axel Paulson

Biellman spin—a spin maneuver named after Swiss skater Denise Biellman

crescendo—the peak of a gradual increase, especially in the loudness of music

resolve—firmness of purpose

rhinestones—a colorless imitation diamond of high luster made usually of glass or paste

taunt—to provoke or challenge in a mocking or insulting manner

toe loop—one of the simplest jumps; done with a toe pick-assisted takeoff that lands on the same backward outside edge

toe pick—the teeth at the front of a skate blade that assist a skater in jumps and spins

DISCUSSION QUESTIONS

1. Maggie and Beatrice are twin sisters who both ice skate, but their styles and personalities differ greatly. Do you have siblings or friends who are different than you?

2. Maggie and her mother often disagree. What problems come up when parents and children disagree? Is there a good way to resolve these sorts of disagreements?

3. Music plays a role in helping Maggie express her feelings. Why do you think this is? What besides music helps people express feelings?

WRITING PROMPTS

1. Re-write the scene in which the twins first meet Coach Stone this time from Beatrice's perspective.

2. Write an extra scene in which Maggie and Beatrice go to watch Coach Stone perform in a skating exhibition.

MORE ABOUT
ICE SKATING

Ice skating was said to be brought to North America from Europe in the 1740s. Speed skating and hockey soon developed after ice skating appeared.

Ice skating first appeared in the Olympic Games in 1908. The Games were held in London that year, and competitions in figure skating were held for women, men, and pairs.

The toe pick is a jagged edge on the tip of skating blades. Figure skaters use toe picks to stop or pivot by digging the edge into the ice.

THE FUN DOESN'T STOP HERE!

FIND MORE AT:
CAPSTONEKIDS.COM

Authors and Illustrators | Videos and Contests
Games and Puzzles | Heroes and Villains

Find cool websites and
more books like this one at
www.facthound.com

Just type in the Book ID:
9781496549273
and you're ready to go!